KIKI AND
FRIENDS

The Circus is Coming to Town

Also in the Kiki and Friends series

by Francesca Hepton

A Case of Mistaken Identity

A Day at the Races

The Major

Picture book

Kiki the Kung Fu Kitten

KIKI AND
FRIENDS

The Circus is Coming to Town

FRANCESCA HEPTON

Babili Books

ISBN: 978-1-9999126-8-0

www.kikiandfriends.co.uk

To all you amazing superheroes

out there – yes, YOU!

Kiki and Friends

Lord Byron
Kiki
Banjo
Poe
Edgar
Tiny + Titch
Allan

Miro
Picasso
Cezanne
"The Rat Pack"

The Farmies

Contents

Chapter 1

Big News

BANJO WAS WAVING a leaflet wildly around in the air when he came racing out into the back garden. Kiki was busy reading on the patio with Dali the resident mouse artist who was giving her a few tips. Kiki always wanted to learn how to do things better.

In this case, Kiki wanted to understand the *Cats' Code of Conduct*. It was an ancient manuscript The Wise One had given to her after their first adventure with his sons: Edgar, Allan and Poe. Together they had outwitted that bad lot of cats: the Farmies. "The Wise One" wasn't his real name, it was Lord Byron. Such a grand sounding name for a grand man. And he sure knew a thing or two about life.

Reading through the rules, Kiki didn't notice Banjo jumping around excitedly. She was totally focused on learning how cats had managed to be lazy for so long. The ancient manuscript also explained why humans just did everything for cats:

It was important for Kiki to learn the secret Cats' Code of Conduct – CCC – so she could share it with her best friend Banjo, who had a real talent for getting into trouble.

At that moment she noticed Banjo. He was jumping from one paw to the other as if he were standing on hot coals and had ants in his pants. "Oooh! Oooh!" he kept gasping, desperate to get their attention. Dali understood he wasn't going to get any further in teaching Kiki with Banjo wheezing to the point of almost exploding. Dali sighed in defeat and turned his disapproving little eyes to Banjo. He didn't notice Dali impatiently fold his little arms.

Banjo was red in the face with excitement.

"Zingalingalanglong and tickle my orange belly pink. You'll never guess the great news I have. Betcha, betcha, you can't guessa!" Banjo teased.

"The circus is coming to town." Dali said dryly.

"Well you know how to ruin a cat's moment!" Banjo grumbled. how did you guess?" Dali looked at the flyer Banjo was clutching in his sweaty paw.

"Oh!, well anyway. Look, Kiki!" He threw a brightly coloured advert down in front of Kiki. Determined not to let smarty-pants Dali ruin his mood. "It was delivered today." He was still jumping from one paw to the other.

"The circus is coming. The circus is coming to Sleepy Meadow. The circus is coming here." He looked like he was going to burst at any moment. "Never in my entire life has the circus come to Sleepy Meadow!"

Kiki opened up the bright orange and red leaflet. There were pictures of people on the trapeze, acrobats in mid-air, clowns juggling, belly-dancers and elephants stacked up on top of each other.

"I've never been to a circus," she said. "What's it all about?"

"What do you mean what's it all about?" asked Banjo, wide-eyed with disbelief. His fur was on end. How could Kiki be so calm? He stroked his frizzy tail to calm himself. His excitement just couldn't be contained. Skipping around on two paws he sang, "Come to the Circus! Come to the Circus! Boom, boom, la, la! Come on Kiki! It's full of mega-fun, mega-stunts, mega-laughs."

"Well the elephants don't look very happy," said Kiki, still not convinced, but Banjo didn't let it bother him. He continued skipping around using his tail as a microphone: "Come to the circus! Come to the circus! Come on Kiki! It's an amazing experience. Why do you always have to be so serious? I wanted you to come with me."

"Can I come too?" asked Dali. "I would very much like to see the circus. It is very entertaining, Miss Kiki. People do all sorts of clever tricks at the circus. We are sure to have a good laugh with the clowns, too."

"And if it makes you feel any better, it's a real piece of, um, culture," said Banjo, trying to look wise.

"Culture. That's a big word for you, Banjo," teased Dali.

"Well culture, yeah, people used to go to the circus hundreds of years ago. They had bearded ladies and really tall men on stilts and the taming of the lion. But now..."

"Taming lions!" shrieked Kiki. "This really isn't sounding good."

Banjo was getting frustrated. He was so excited about the circus. Kiki was ruining it. "Yes, but they probably don't do that at *this* circus. See?" He opened up the leaflet again. "You see, there aren't any pictures of lions. They probably won't have stuff like that or the strongest man in the world, or chained bears on bikes..."

"Chained bears," shrieked Kiki again. "Why do they do that? Bears belong in the wild with the elephants and lions."

"Yes, but there aren't any bears here." He waved the leaflet in her face again. "Come on, it'll be fun."

"Okay," Kiki agreed in the end. She didn't want to disappoint her best friend. Besides, it *did* look fun.

"I'll go tell the boys," said Dali, rushing off. "Tiny and Titch, Winston and Churchill are sure to want to come." He dashed off inside the house.

"Well since we're making a day of it," said Banjo, "why don't we invite Piero? He must be bored all alone."

"Some-body-a say-a my name!" Piero's head popped over the fence.

"Have you been there the entire time?" asked Banjo.

"Ah well-a, how do you English say? I was-a just-a passing."

"Yeah, sure," said Banjo. "Come on over since you're here." Piero swung swiftly over the fence in one jump. He was still wearing his diamante collar and matching anklet and ring.

"Piero, you really draw attention to yourself with all that jewellery," said Banjo.

"I like-a shiny things," he replied, polishing up his little ring. "So, when-a do we go-a to the circus-eo?"

"You were listening in," Banjo said.

"May-a-be I heard-a few things about-a mega-fun and a circus-eo. I went-a to a circus-eo in bella Italia once. It was fabuloso."

"You see Kiki, it'll be fun," said Banjo, getting excited again. "We're bound to have a blast."

"When is it?" asked Kiki. Banjo looked closely at the leaflet.

"Not sure."

"Well, *where* is it then?" she asked.

Banjo looked closely at the leaflet.

"Not sure."

“What is-a the matter with you-o?” asked Piero. “Do you need-a glasses?”

“Er, um,” Banjo stuttered.

“Or may-abe you cannota read-eo! Ha, ha!”

Banjo hemmed and hawed, scuffling his paws along the edge of the patio.

“No, well,” he mumbled looking embarrassed. “I’ve never learnt how to read.”

“Ha, ha, ha,” Piero laughed loudly. “A cat at your age that cannot read-eo, I never heard of anything-so ridiculoso in my life-a.”

“It’s not my fault,” Banjo blurted out defensively. “My parents never taught me. They were too busy catching mice.” Dali clutched his little mouse throat and gulped. “Don’t worry Dali, they were naughty mice.” Dali sighed in relief

“Ah, I’m-a sorreo, Banjo. I didn’t know-eo you couldn’t readeo.” Piero was sorry for having laughed at Banjo. He put a comforting paw on his shoulder to apologise.

Kiki was surprised Banjo couldn’t read.

"Don't worry Banjo, after Dali has taught me a bit more, I'll teach you using big writing."

"Thanks Kiki, you're a real pal."

"Now let me see..." She took the leaflet from him. "It says that it's on for three days this weekend and it starts on Saturday. Well, that's today. And it's being held on the school playing field."

"Do you think Edgar, Allan and Poe will want to come?" asked Banjo.

"They're visiting their Great Aunt Mildred in Cottontail Valley," replied Kiki.

"That sounds like a bundle of laughs," chuckled Banjo. "Not!"

"I guess-a it's just us three and-a the leetle guyz," said Piero.

"Can we go today; can we go now?" asked Banjo, jumping up and down again in excitement. "We'll sneak into the big marquee, the Big Top – nobody'll notice us."

"If we go today, we need to leave in about two hours. That'll give us enough time to get there before it starts," declared Kiki.

"And-a that'll give meo just enough time-eo to comb and style-eo my hair-eo," said Piero. "I look such a mess-eo." He didn't have a whisker out of place. His fur was purrfectly sleeked down. What could he possibly do for two hours?

"Don't leave without-a meo," shouted Piero as he jumped elegantly back over the fence.

Chapter 2

The Big Top

PIERO TURNED UP bang on time (as usual). He looked exactly the same as he did before (as usual). "That's cool," said Banjo, who was more than ready to have fun at the circus.

Dali had changed. He'd put on his special shiny red shoes and a different neckerchief. It was a polka-dot red one with white spots.

"I've not seen that neckerchief before," Kiki commented. "So what mood are you in when you wear that one?"

"Spotty red means I am ready for anything, to have fun, no rules, no questions asked."

Tiny and Titch turned up wearing their matching black beanies and Winston and Churchill arrived in their bowler hats, but they had little umbrellas now, too.

"You never know how the weather may turn," said Winston.

"Yes," agreed Churchill. "It may start raining cats and dogs before we get there."

"*Hope for the best and prepare for the worst* – that's our motto."

Banjo shook his head. Those two little mice were always full of the weirdest sayings. They talked gobbledegook half the time. But raining cats and dogs had to be the weirdest one yet. "When did it last rain cats and dogs? Where was I ? Why do I always miss these things?"

He sighed and Kiki patted him on his slumped shoulders, explaining that raining cats and dogs just meant heavy rain.

"Oh of course, I knew that. I mean it would really hurt if lots of poodles started falling out of the sky." Banjo went red for the second time that morning.

"Come on-eo, Banjo, what-a are we-a waiting for-a. This was your-a great idea-o, let's-a go have some fun-eo."

"Right on Piero, you said it." Churchill climbed up onto Kiki.

Banjo and Piero were in front and the rest of the mice clambered onto Kiki for a ride. There was no way their little legs would have been able to keep up. And there was no way they'd be able to get on Piero's back without slipping off with all that gel. On Banjo's back – well, they'd get lost in his jungle of fur.

After a little walk, they finally saw the Big Top on the school playing field. There were lots of brightly coloured stalls, wagons and people in costumes juggling hoops and others blowing flames from their mouths.

"Wow, it's paw-some!" exclaimed Banjo. "Come on, let's go."

They ran the rest of the way, the little mice holding onto Kiki's fur for dear life, Winston and Churchill holding onto their bowler hats.

They snuck around the back of the big marquee unnoticed. Lots of people were queuing at the front entrance where the jugglers were. The queue was mostly parents with young children holding boxes of popcorn and candyfloss from the nearby stalls.

"I think we're a bit early," said Kiki. "Maybe we could take a look around before it starts."

All the caravans belonging to the performers were parked around the back of the marquee. Some were modern caravans; some were wooden, traditional ones painted the old-fashioned way.

Kiki and friends poked their heads through the open windows. They were full of costumes, props, make-up and a general mess. They found one where the lady trapeze artists in glittering swim costumes and feather headbands were still busy putting on their make-up.

The caravan next door to them was wobbling around like a bucking bronco. This was the clowns' caravan.

Inside were clowns dressed in silly costumes, with oversized feet and big red noses. They were jumping on each other, pulling flags out of hats, squirting water out of flowers, popping ping pong balls in and out of their mouths and firing them like missiles at each other.

"Looks like they're having fun," Kiki said.

"You see, the circus is a fun place!" Banjo said in an *I told you so* kind of way.

"Look over there." Kiki pointed to a gigantic shed that had the word ELEPHANTS above it. "That's where the elephants are kept. Can we go see? We've got loads of time. The queue to get in the Big Top is still really long."

"Yeah, why not," Banjo agreed.

Along the way they passed clowns on monocycles practicing for the show, men with enormous moustaches standing on enormous balls whilst juggling stripy batons.

They even saw some children stacked on top of each other's shoulders to spell out the word WELCOME.

"What did I tell you Kiki, this is mega-amazing!" Banjo grinned. But the front door to the elephant shed was locked.

"Never mind," said Kiki as they started to walk back to the main tent, "there's lots more stuff we can look at—"

"Oh no!" yelled Banjo a little too loudly. "It's the Farmies."

Not again, thought Kiki.

Sure enough, lurking behind the Clown Caravan were the Farmies. The lazy, greedy cats Kiki and her friends had tricked the week before. The mean triplets were there along with the doddery tabby Miro, his thick black wonky line above his eyes making him look even more confused than the Kiki remembered.

Moments later, the leader of the Farmies, Picasso, appeared. He was a little white grandpappy with a scowl scratched across his face and droopy eyes.

"Uh-oh, are those the guyza you tried to trick and send arounda to my hous-eo?"

"Yes, but I'm so glad we didn't," Banjo said, feeling bad.

"Me too-eo," Piero said, taking a gulp and running his finger around his diamante collar as if it had all of a sudden become a little too tight.

The Farmies lived on the outskirts of the village of Sleepy Meadow at Murk Farm. They were a bad bunch. Not the kind to invite around to your Great Aunt Mildred's for tea.

Part of their posse was the Rat Pack, who were all wearing black sunglasses and looking like they were ready to do something naughty. Two mean-looking rats stood behind the leader of the Rat Pack, Cezanne, who was the first to spot Kiki. Cezanne shouted:

"Hey, ain't that the crazy gal that gave us the run around?"

"Yeah," sneered Percy, the meanest of the mean triplets, who remembered Kiki had made him look like a fool before tying up the Rat Pack by their tails.

"My tail's still sore," sneered Cezanne, "and I'm going to make sure she knows about it."

They stomped their way towards Kiki.

"Blimey," said Banjo. "They're coming straight for us. Run for it!"

Kiki didn't want to put her friends in danger even though she could have probably handled the lot of them right there and then. She led her friends back in the direction of the Elephant Shed with the mice holding on even tighter to her fur, literally flying horizontal in the wind. Dali's little shiny red shoes were flapping behind him. The Farmies were hot on their tails.

They found a crack in between the planks of the Elephant Shed and slipped in. It was very quiet, empty and pitch black.

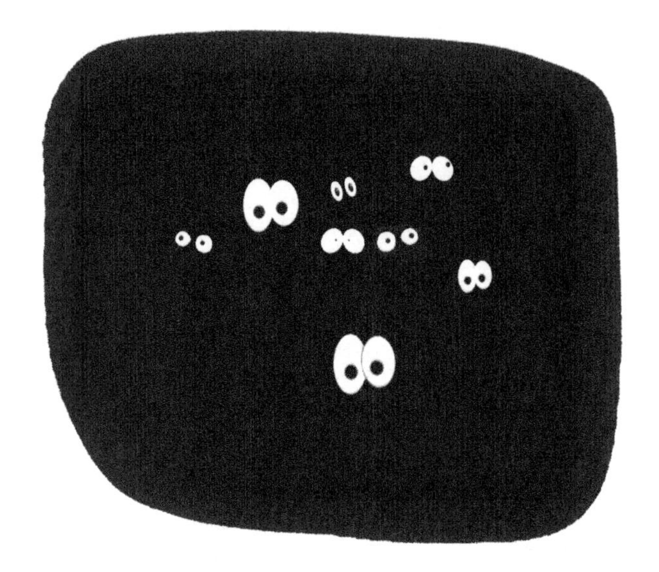

"Where are the elephants?" asked Tiny. "I can't see them—"

"—but I can smell them," Titch said. "Pooey."

"I don't know," said Dali. "Wait! I can hear something."

"You lot wait here. I'll go check what it is," Kiki said, protective as ever.

The rest of them waited in the dark room, trying not to cough despite the really strong whiff of elephant dung. They listened as the Farmies ran past the shed.

"You look over there," ordered the bossy little Picasso. "We'll look in the caravans."

"Can you see anything?" Banjo whispered.

"No, it's a too darkeo. I hope those two hurry upeo or I'm-a gonna start smelling like elephant dung-eo."

"Don't worry Piero. Nothing could get past your fur gel," Banjo laughed.

Kiki came rushing back.

"There's something going on in the back room. That's where the noise is coming from. Sounds like a party. If we stay in the shadows, we won't be seen. Follow me."

Everyone followed, except Winston and Churchill who rushed ahead.

Banjo stumbled through the dark, tripping over some heavy chains on the floor and then some really tiny chains. Kiki picked up the tiny chains. "Hm, I wonder what these are for."

"Small monsters. It's spooky in here," Banjo said. He knew Kiki would tease him and call him a scaredy-cat, so he said it first. "But I'm not being a scaredy-cat."

Somebody else in the shed was scared, though. There was a little baby mouse crying in the far corner. Her eyes were red, she was snivelling.

"Mummy, mummy," she cried.

"She's just a little whippersnapper," said Dali. He tried to talk to her, but she ran away when Banjo came close and then Winston and Churchill came running back.

"What ho, chaps," said Winston, catching his breath, "You are not going to believe your eyes when you see this."

"Follow us, chaps," said Churchill. "We'll be safe soon."

It gradually became lighter the closer they got to the next large room. Kiki had a little look around in the darkness behind her, but the little scared mouse was nowhere to be seen.

Winston and Churchill were right. As they got through the door, they couldn't believe their eyes. Right in front of them was a miniature circus for cats. They stayed hidden in the shadows by the wall.

"Wow!" Banjo exclaimed. "Just like a real circus."

There was a circus ring with a trampoline and trapeze stuff for the acrobats, and seats encircling it for the audience. But they didn't see any excited little children sitting there. Instead, the seats were filled with excited cats. Cats of all kinds, ages and colours.

"How are they going to perform on such a tiny trampoline?" Banjo asked in wonder.

His question was soon answered as the ringmaster walked out into the middle. It was a white mouse with an extremely tall hat and a little waistcoat.

"Welcome, welcome to the Incredible Circus of Mice!"

There was lots of cheering from the cats.

"We have a fabulous line-up for you today. We promise you'll have a ball. But not a *fur* ball."

The cats in the audience laughed.

"So just sit back, relax and let's bring in the clowns!"

The little clowns were also mice. They had little (but big for them) red noses and funny wigs and big floppy black shoes. They were juggling little balls in their little paws whilst cycling on monocycles. One was going around hitting the others with a rubbery bat, making them fall off. All the cats were laughing.

Little mice with trays were walking around the audience selling popcorn and drinks, just like in the real circus, but with extra treats like catnip and cream sticks, too. There was a slightly bigger mouse with a big moustache and tight-fitting costume. He was flexing his muscles to impress the cats.

"Must be the strong-mouse instead of the strongman," Banjo said, pointing.

"He looks just like you, Dali," Titch laughed.

"Thanking you kindly, he does not," Dali huffed with his hands on his hips.

Other mice came out into the ring in shiny little costumes. They balanced on top of each other's shoulders until just one little mouse at the bottom was holding up twenty other mice.

The tiny tower of mice was met with thundering cheers and clapping.

Kiki remembered that they were supposed to be hiding from the Farmies. She looked around the room. Her tail frizzy and twitchy in anticipation.

On the far side of the room she spotted a scruffy looking grey cat with a patch over his eye. He noticed her looking at him and stared back at her before slinking behind the curtains where the performing mice were coming from.

"You lot stay here in the shadows until I come back. If the coast is clear, we can make a run for the big tent. There are more places to hide there."

The four little mice clambered back onto Kiki to get a better view as she searched the rest of the elephant shed.

"Wot?" Banjo said, only half listening to Kiki. He was unable to tear his eyes away from the little mice on the trapeze flying through the air, spinning around and then being caught by another mouse swinging on a trapeze. Kiki rolled her eyes.

"It's-a okay, Kiki, I heard-a what you said-eo. I will keep my eyes-a on him-a until you get-a back-eo."

"Thanks Piero."

"Oh and-a Kiki, be careful-a."

Kiki was touched by his concern.

"We'll come with you, Miss Kiki," said Winston.

"We'll protect you," said Titch.

"—and we'll come too," added Tiny. "We're small."

"They won't see us." Titch finished off his sentence.

Chapter 3

Mission Mouse

PROWLING IN THE DARKNESS, Kiki switched to her night vision. Away from the laughter and noise of the Incredible Circus of Mice, she could hear something else. It sounded like screaming.

"No sign of the Farmies," said Kiki.

"Affirmative," said Winston.

"Copy that," said Churchill.

Because of Winston and Churchill's military ways, Kiki felt like she was on a mission.

"Permission to investigate that screaming sound," she said.

"Permission granted," said Winston. Everyone nodded in agreement. This was serious stuff.

The screams got louder and more disturbing. It sounded like someone or something was in real pain.

When Kiki peered around the corner, she saw the evil eye-patch cat. He was standing in a small room with sawdust on the floor and a single light bulb hanging from the ceiling. He had an evil grin and a whip in his hand. He cracked his whip to the ground. *Thwack.*

"No, no, please don't make us do it," came a small squeaky voice from the darkness. It was a mouse dressed in a grey elephant costume.

"Don't you dare backchat me," thundered the eye-patch cat. "We 'ave a circus to run and you will perform as I say."

The whip slapped the floor again. *Thwack.*There were lots of squeals from the other mice wearing the same grey outfits.

"Now put your trunks on and get out there!"

"But we can barely breathe in them," complained another really skinny looking mouse.

"You are tryin' my patience."

Thwack.

The trembling little mice did as he said and put on their trunks. This transformed them into a herd of mini elephants.

They trudged out through the curtains into the circus ring followed by the eye-patch cat. Kiki could hear the cats clapping and shouting excitedly: "It's the elephants, it's the elephants!"

She could also hear the rattling of chains. Out of the circle of light created by the single light bulb, lots of little "elephant" mice, maybe twenty in total, were chained to the walls in the tiny chains.

"Oh, my goodness!" Kiki couldn't help but gasp in horror.

"This is unacceptable," declared Winston.

"We must get the others instantly and save our fellow mice," said Churchill.

This time there was no need for them to plan anything. They had to save the poor "elephant" mice.

Kiki ran back to the Incredible Circus of Mice.

Banjo was still hypnotised by the show. The trunks and sparkling tiaras hid the frowns of the little elephant mice. The audience loved watching them walk on balls and jump through flaming hoops of fire.

"Banjo," Kiki shook him out of his hypnotic state. "Banjo, we've got to go!"

"But they're so cute." Banjo didn't want to leave.

"Now, Banjo, now!"

Nobody argued with Kiki when she gave orders. Banjo knew something bad must be up.

They sped back to the chained elephant mice.

Banjo was shocked to see the tiny bodies chained to the wall. A tear swelled in his eye.

"I need you to help break the chains," Dali said, trying to pull them apart until the veins were bulging out of his head. It looked like his eyeballs would pop out first.

"We must save them," said Dali, putting all of his might into trying to break one of the chains himself. It was too hard. He kept trying.

"Leave-a that-a to Banjo and Kiki," said Piero. "You and the others lead-a the cutesy miceez outsideo."

The little mouse that had been snivelling in the darkness came running in.

"Mummy, mummy!" Nose and whiskers twitching, she hugged one of the newly freed mice. Her little arms barely long enough to go around her waist.

"I'm going to have to ask you to hurry, ma'am," said Winston who was filing the mice out of the elephant shed military style with the help of Churchill, Tiny and Titch. Some of the poor circus mice could only shuffle themselves out of danger.

Suddenly the eye-patch cat turned up from behind the curtains. Perhaps he'd heard the little mouse cry out for her mother.

"Wot is goin' on?" he snarled. "I won't stand for this."

"You carry on, Banjo. I'll deal with Mister Bad Pants here," said Kiki.

"Ha," scoffed the eye-patch cat. "A scrawny little fing like you! You don't stand a chance against me. I'm as 'ard as nails."

"And I'm as slick as cream," said Kiki tying on her headband.

"Oh yeah? You and whose army? You brought your bandages I see. You're gonna need 'em."

His threats didn't upset Kiki one bit. "This is no bandage; this is my headband of power so watch out Mister Bad Pants."

She tied her headband firmly in place and took up her cat stance. She was ready for anything.

"Piero, go get the other elephant mice left in the ring, but don't make it obvious what you're doing otherwise we'll have a hundred cats after us and not just the Farmies."

"He's not goin' anywhere." The eye-patch cat started to make for Piero. But Kiki moved swiftly into action. She leapt through the air and landed in front of the eye-patch cat, blocking his way.

"Out ov my way, scrawny cat," he snarled. "You ave bovered me enuff."

"Well how about I cheer you up instead?" jibed Kiki. Behind her, Piero dove through the curtains into the circus ring.

Kiki moved her paws so quickly back and forth, up and down, round and round, they soon became a blur. The eye-patch cat was watching her moves and became dizzy from all the whizzing of her paws. He couldn't see past them to get to Kiki, nor could he see where to hit because of her blinding speed.

Kiki's super-fast moves were hypnotising him. He shook his head and snapped out of the trance.

"Stop prattin' around and fight propa, like a real cat," he snarled.

"Oh, and you think that picking on little mice that aren't even the size of your paw, in chains, is fighting properly? Not to mention the whip."

He looked down at his whip as if he just remembered he had it. "Ha ha! I 'ave you now." He cracked his whip against the ground. *Thwack*. It curled and flailed like a long black snake.

Kiki was not put off by the whip, though she had never come up against one before. Everything froze in time and space. It was a standoff. Leaping like a panther, Kiki flew through the air. She let out a mighty cry that made the eye-patch cat wince. He tried to move out of her way, but Kiki was already upon him.

Like lightning, she grabbed the end of the whip in mid-air. Almost as soon as she dropped to the ground she somersaulted over his head and then ran around him. Round and round and round she sped, until he was all tied up in his whip, tottering like a spinning top.

Chapter 4

Piero's Mission

WHEN PIERO HAD gone out into the circus ring, he was not sure what he was going to do. How could he get the little performing elephant mice out of there without drawing attention to himself?

"Helloo-eo everyone-eo," he began. All the cats in the audience started laughing.

"What-a is so funny-eo?" He genuinely didn't understand that they were laughing at the way he spoke. They thought it was another circus act.

"Are you all having a good-a time-eo?"

The cats shouted back in unison. "Yes-eo!"

He finally twigged. This was going to be quite fun.

"So, you all-a think that-a I speak-a funny-eo?"

"Yes-eo!" they all shouted back again.

"Well-a I give you all a chAllange, right-eo?"

"Right-eo!"

"You all have-a to sing the Musica Man song-a for me. I'll-a start-a for those of you who do not-a know-a it:

I say: I am the music man, and I come from far away-o and I can play-o!

And you say-o: What can you play-o?

Then I say-o: I play-a the piano!

And you sing: Pia-pia-pia-no, pia-no, pia-no; pia-pia-pia-no, pia-pia-no."

The cats rolled over in their seats, positively purring with laughter.

"Right-a, we start-a and you can all-a sound like meo! I am the musico man, and I come from far away-o and I can play-o!"

"What can you play-o?" sang all the cats at the top of their lungs.

"I play-a the piano!"

Whilst the audience was singing the chorus, "Pia-pia-pia-no, pia-no, pia-no; pia-pia-pia-no, pia-pia-no," Piero whispered to all the mice that they were being rescued.

At first the mice were afraid, but then they thought that since nothing could be worse than what they had already gone though, they started to leave the ring. Piero then went back to his very excited singing audience.

"Very good-eo, now you sound like me-o!" Piero was having a great time.

And the crowd of cats was yowling with joy. He started the song again, waved his arms in the air like a conductor.

"*I am the musico man, and I come from far away-o and I can play-o!*"

"What can you play-o?" melodiously mewled all the cats.

"*I play-a the piano!*" sang Piero.

Everyone joined in with the chorus: "Pia-pia-pia-no, pia-no, pia-no; pia-pia-pia-no, pia-pia-no."

Before the cats could finish the chorus for a third time, Banjo appeared from behind the curtains, grabbed Piero by his diamante collar and whipped him out of the ring.

Thinking this was all part of the act, the cats started laughing, watching big furry Banjo dragging the sleek Piero out of the ring by his sparkling collar.

Once out the back, Piero asked, "Did it work-eo?"

"You were fantastic," purred Kiki.

The eye-patch cat had woken up. He tugged against the chains.

"You'll not get away wiv vis. Them others will come and find you." He tugged against the whip wrapped around him. He couldn't break free.

The roar of the crowd was so loud it drowned out the eye-patch cat's shouting. Kiki stuffed an elephant-mouse costume in his mouth.

"I don't think you'll be going anywhere," said Banjo. He pulled his eye-patch and let it snap back onto his face.

"Ow, mat urt," mumbled the eye-patch cat through the grey fabric.

"Good," replied Banjo. "Stop being a bully. Bet you wouldn't be so brave in front of real elephants. Pick on someone your own size in future."

They left him there and joined the others outside.

The thin and sad looking elephant mice were so confused as to what was going on, they hadn't even run away.

Winston spoke to them, tipping his bowler hat. "You have to run now, friends. Find a new place to live."

The little herd of mice peeled off their grey costumes and scampered off across the school playing field. They scurried to freedom and a new life away from the circus.

Chapter 5

The Great Escape

AFTER THE ELEPHANT mice had gone, Kiki felt a lot happier, but still a little worried about the Farmies.

"We're not out of dangerous waters yet, my friends," said Churchill.

"What on earth are you talking about, Churchill?" asked Banjo. "We're not in any kind of water."

He looked around him in search of puddles or a pond.

"What he means, Banjo, is the Farmies are still looking for us," explained Kiki.

"Oooh!" said Banjo slowly, still trying to understand what the water had to do with it. "I don't know, all I wanted was to come to the circus, and we've found poor elephant mice, now there's dangerous water somewhere and then, then we've got the Farmies, ooh, Farmies, Farmies!"

Banjo was then pointing and shrieking. "Farmies, Farmies, Farmies!"

"Yes, we know what they are called," said Dali. "No need to repeat yourself."

"No, he means Farmies at 12 o'clock," said Winston.

"I don't mean at 12 o'clock," yelled Banjo. "I mean NOW and dead ahead coming right for us."

Dali didn't even have time to shake his little head – he'd have to explain that one to Banjo later – as Kiki scooped him up, running as fast as as lightning.

"Split up and head for the Big Top," Kiki shouted. "We can hide in the crowd; they wouldn't do anything in there."

Kiki knew most of the Farmies would come after her since she had made such fools of them when she locked them in the barn last time. But she couldn't risk being seen "in action" in front of all these people.

As it says in the Cat Code of Conduct, it is the sacred duty of all cats to make sure humans never find out just how clever they are – otherwise they'd put them to work. The thought of losing their freedom and time to laze in the sun or in front of the fire was too much to bear.

They split up as Kiki suggested. Kiki carried Dali and the others on her back. She headed slightly away from the Big Top. She wanted to stop off at the Clown Wagon first. The mean triplets – Percy, Bysshe, Shelley – and the Rat Pack followed her.

Piero dashed into one of the traditional circus wagons completely unnoticed.

Picasso and Miro chased Banjo right into the Big Top. The show in the Big Top circus tent had started. Bearded ladies dressed as belly dancers were about to go on.

Banjo quietly stole a veil that was next to one of the dancers complaining about a sprained ankle.

"But I can't go on," she said to the Ringmaster, pulling off her fake beard. "Me ankle really 'urts!" She was about to pick up her veil before stomping off (with a limp, of course), when she noticed it was gone.

"Where's me veil? Who stole me veil?" she wailed.

"Well that does it," said the Ringmaster in his enormously tall top hat and smart tuxedo suit. "You can't go on now. You don't have a veil." He went out into the ring to introduce the next act. When the clapping stopped he announced, "And now ladies and gentlemen, may I introduce you to our lovely Bearded Belles Belly Dancers!"

Banjo put the long veil over his face and followed the dozen other belly dancers out into the ring. He looked behind him and saw Picasso thump his fist and kick up the soil before turning to Miro to blame him for letting Banjo get away.

Banjo was pleased with himself, but quickly realised what was about to happen. He was going to have to belly dance in front of all these children looking at him with their mouths full of popcorn and candyfloss.

The other ladies got into position. He squatted down next to them. Then the music started. He wasn't sure what to do. They just seemed to be wiggling a lot; he started to shake his hips from side to side. His large belly wobbled along in time. Some of the children were pointing and laughing at him.

"Look mummy, that lady's got a really furry belly," said one.

"Look, that lady's got a really wobbly tummy," said another.

The audience started laughing, thinking he was part of the act. The other belly dancers did not like being upstaged. They kept staring at Banjo. As one lady was doing her solo act and Banjo was wobbling his belly around with the rest of them at the back, really quite enjoying himself, a gruff looking bearded lady asked him:

"Who are you?"

"Meow," said Banjo, forgetting to put on a human voice.

"Well, Mia whoever you are, you are not part of our dance show."

She picked him up with her muscly arms and threw him to the side of the ring. The audience howled with laughter.

Oh, why couldn't I have been caught up with the clowns, he thought. Then he had a bright idea. He kept on wobbling around as much as he could, whilst sneaking over the side of the ring.

He picked up one of the snack trays and pretended to serve the audience with popcorn. That would keep the Farmies away. As long as he was with people, they couldn't get to him. He just had to wait for Kiki to turn up and save the day.

Kiki was busy getting into a clown outfit in the Clown Wagon. She made sure she put her headband on underneath. Dali and the others hid in her large, green wig. She followed all the other clowns out of the wagon, trying not to trip over the gigantic floppy shoes she was wearing.

The troop of clowns made their way to the Big Top.

Bysshe, the dopier of the three mean triplets, was waiting outside the clown wagon with Percy and Shelley – who was already daydreaming.

"I bet she's one of those clowns," said Percy. "Don't let them out of your sight," he said, nudging Shelley who woke with a start.

The three of them moved into position and waited behind the curtain of the circus ring. The Ringmaster yelled: "And now for the Funnies!"

There was no way the triplets could follow the clowns now.

The audience clapped and the clowns ran in. They immediately started juggling, pulling silly faces, knocking each other out and squirting the audience with their humongous fake flowers. Kiki knew she couldn't just stand there in the circus ring, so she started doing some of her kung-fu moves.

"Hold on tight, boys," she whispered to her wig.

She twirled and somersaulted, did handstands and backflips. Dali and the others held on really tight.

"I'm feeling a little sea-sick," said Dali.

"We must weather the storm," said Winston in his usual military way.

Kiki spotted Banjo in the audience. Even though he looked completely ridiculous with his glittering veil, she would recognise him anywhere. She gave him a wink. Banjo recognised her in the silly clown outfit. He smiled back, relieved to see her.

"And now, the moment you have all been waiting for," said the Ringmaster. "The Elephant Parade!"

Elephants, thought Kiki. *I thought there weren't going to be any elephants.* She remembered how sad the mice elephants had been.

A man with an eye-patch led the majestic elephants out into the ring. He had a whip.

Eye-patch cat and now an eye-patch man!!! thought Kiki. *It's happening all over again.*

"We have to save the elephants," Kiki whispered into her wig.

"Aren't we in enuff bovver, Miss, without savin the elephants?" asked Tiny.

"We 'ave to save ourselves too, Miss," added Titch.

"It may seem impossible, friends, but when have I ever failed you?" There was no reply. Kiki was right. "We're not leaving here without those elephants."

The sad-looking elephants trudged into the ring. The clowns started flicking ping pong balls at them and pretended to run away, scared.

Kiki looked around to assess the situation. Percy, Bysshe, Shelley and the Rat Pack were hiding behind the curtain. Percy had a wicked smile.

"I'm going to get you," he mouthed to Kiki.

Oh no you're not, thought Kiki. *I'm too fast for the likes of you.*

"Dali, Winston, Churchill, Tiny and Titch, I want you to go tell the elephants to stampede out of the tent when they hear a big bang. They have to head for the school car park."

"What crazy cat-brained idea do you have in mind?" asked Dali.

"Just wait and see." Kiki smiled. "When you finish delivering the message, come back to me."

"What if we're spotted?" asked Dali.

"You're too small," said Kiki. "Besides, everyone is enjoying the show too much to be bothered or notice anything strange going on."

"But I fought elephants was scared of mice," said Titch.

"You've been watching too much TV," said Kiki.

Since there were no more questions and they knew Kiki had never failed them, they carried out their orders.

Some of the elephants did seem a bit bothered by the mice, but it was only because Tiny and Titch were tickling them in their big ears when they whispered the message.

Once the mice had all returned into Kiki's clown wig, she made her way over to the cannon.

"I'm going to hide you in this, um, bucket for now, then I'll make a big bang noise. That'll be the signal to head for the car park. Make sure to cover your ears. If anything goes wrong, head for the car park."

The mice could not see that Kiki was stuffing them into the cannon. She didn't have a choice. If she was going to have to fight the Farmies, she didn't want her little mice friends to be in any danger. She moved the cannon around to the front of the marquee, for their explosive escape.

Percy couldn't see what she was doing, either. He was getting angrier by the minute, but there was nothing he could do in a tent full of people.

"I say," said Winston. "This is a really deep bucket."

Well that takes care of the Farmies, thought Kiki gratefully.

"WOT?" shouted Titch, because he had his paws over his ears.

Kiki gave a secret wave to Banjo to say the big moment was about to come.

She lit the fuse...

Five little mice with their paws covering their ears flew over the audience straight out of the marquee. The audience cheered at this surprise event. But they were in for an even bigger surprise. The elephants started to stampede out of the front of the marquee as well. People jumped up from their seats, running in all directions.

Kiki made a run for it too. She grabbed Banjo on her way out. Once outside, Kiki jumped onto an elephant, dragging Banjo through the air with her.

The car park was a few hundred metres away. Kiki looked behind her. It was complete chaos; people were running everywhere, and the Ringmaster was on the loudspeaker. "Stay calm, stay in your seats, it's all part of the big show," he boomed, although he didn't sound very convincing.

Everybody was crying out, "Stampede! Stampede!"

The Farmies were all running behind them now, pushing through the legs of the mad crowd of people who were walking around like headless chickens.

The groundsmen of the circus spotted the Farmies.

"It was those pesky cats that scared the elephants, after them, catch them!"

Well that takes care of the Farmies, thought Kiki gratefully.

When they finally got to the car park, the five mice were looking a little cross and a little burnt.

"Why didn't you tell us you were going to blast us to kingdom come?" asked Dali. His usually pristinely twirled black moustache was fried and frizzled and smoking at the ends.

"You're wearing your polka dot neckerchief, Dali. I thought anything goes!" Kiki smiled.

"Yes, I must say Miss Kiki, it was bit of a rough landing," said Tiny rubbing his head.

"Not if you come prepared," said Winston as he glided down slowly on his umbrella, which he and Churchill had used as a parachute.

"Glad you're all safe," said Kiki.

"Yes, we're all here and so is this HERD OF ELEPHANTS!" said Banjo. "What are we going to do about them?"

The grateful elephants had gathered around Kiki and her friends.

"Just a minute, wait, where's Piero?" asked Kiki. "Anyone seen Piero?"

"Not since we rescued the elephant mice," said Banjo.

They looked back to the Big Top. Walking towards them was a man on stilts.

"Oh no! He's coming straight for us. We've been caught!" cried Dali.

"I don't fink so," smiled Titch.

"What are you-a doing-a with-a all of these elephanteos?" asked the man on stilts.

"Ah Piero, thank goodness you're safe," said Kiki.

"Of courseo. You're not the only one-o with a plan-eo, Kiki," he teased.

"We still have a bit of a big problem," said Banjo, looking at the fifteen or so elephants towering above them, and a baby one. "What are we going to do about them? They're a bit bigger than the mice we rescued."

"That's easy," said Kiki. "Just follow me."

Kiki's friends knew she was clever, but her resourcefulness and calmness never ceased to amaze them. Just what did she intend doing with all these elephants?

Chapter 6

Grandpa George

THE CIRCUS WAS in complete chaos. The police seemed to be more worried about catching the Farmies than catching the elephants. Probably because they wouldn't know how to. They were asking people to calm down and to go back in the tent and watch the show. It was the most memorable circus event ever. One that the residents of Sleepy Meadow would never forget.

Meanwhile, a few blocks down, fifteen grown elephants and a baby elephant with glittering headdresses were being led through the streets by a man on stilts, a green-haired clown and a really furry bearded belly dancer. It wasn't a sight you see every day in Sleepy Meadow.

People either ran indoors and shut the curtains or took pictures of them on their phones. Kiki and the others felt like they were leading a parade.

"The elephants marched down two by two hurrah, hurrah!" sang Banjo.

The elephants followed them without question. They were just pleased to be free from the circus.

"Where are we taking them?" asked Dali. "It's not like they're easy to hide."

"The police-a are sure-a to be after us soon-a," added Piero, who was becoming quite good at walking on his stilts.

"Just trust me on this one," said Kiki calmly. "We're only a few streets away now."

When she finally halted her troop in front of an ordinary looking house, Banjo happily piped up, "I know where we are! This is John's dad's house. Grandpa George. Isn't he a vet?"

"That's right," said Kiki.

"But these elephants don't need a vet; they need a rainforest!" exclaimed Dali. "This is crazy, Kiki."

"Yeah, they're not all going to fit into his house," said Banjo, pointing at the vet's little house.

"Banjo, dear friend," said Dali. "You never cease to amaze me. Of course they are not going to fit in the house. I'm sure that's not what Kiki had in mind."

"Help me get their headdresses off," said Kiki, "and I'll explain."

Kiki then told them the story of how when she was an orphan, someone left her on the steps of Grandpa George's vet clinic. He had taken her in.

The house they were in front of had been her first home. Grandpa George looked after a lot of orphaned animals in his home. She had never seen so many animals in her life. He had gorillas and crocodiles, parakeets, mongoose, squirrels and even a giraffe in the back garden. Grandpa George loved animals. If ever there was anyone to help an animal in need, it was him.

Kiki scribbled a note on a piece of cardboard she found in the neighbour's recycling bin. She found some wire and hung it over one of the elephant's necks.

"That ought to do it. Now, let's find somewhere to hide and see what happens."

They dove into the hedge across the road and parted the leaves just enough so that they could see what was going on in the street.

The elephants sat down on the road and on Grandpa George's lawn. A few people started to gather round. A driver trying to get past beeped his horn.

The sound of the horn woke Grandpa George up. He was dozing on his sofa with a koala under his arm and a snake wrapped around his legs. His glasses were hanging off the end of his big nose.

"What's all the commotion, eh?" he asked the animals that filled his lounge. "Shall we go and see?"

When he got up, he lost his balance because the snake was still coiled around his ankles, but the gorilla caught his arm and steadied him.

He walked over to the window followed by the cheetah, bonobo, duck and all his other curious animals. They peered out of the window and saw fifteen fully-grown elephants and a baby elephant in the front garden and on the street.

"Well my word, oh me oh my, that was not what I was expecting to see." He scuffled across the lounge and put on his shoes. "You lot wait in here; I shan't be long." When he went out the front door, the bonobo slipped between his legs.

"Ah Charlie, always disobeying me."

He moved around the elephants. They didn't seem to be bothered by him.

"Good afternoon, dear chaps. To what do I owe this honour?" he asked the elephants.

The bonobo was sitting on the elephant with the sign, waving and shrieking. Grandpa George went to him. He picked up the sign around its neck.

Grandpa George rubbed his chin in thought. "An elephant who can write, most unusual. Right. There is nothing else for it, we'll call Albert at the Elephant Foundation and get you on your way in no time."

The elephants all trumpeted really loudly. Some of the neighbours were cross. One lady with curlers in her hair and pink fluffy pompoms on her slippers shouted: “George, this is not the Amazon rainforest. You’ve gone too far this time.”

“I agree Mizz Moanalot, it is rather a big problem.” Grandpa George chuckled under his breath. “And actually, elephants usually live in Africa and Asia. Not everything comes from Amazon, my dear.”

Mizz Moanalot did not find it funny. “This is a nice, respectable neighbourhood; these elephants cannot stay here. How will I get my car out of the driveway if there is a great big elephant in the way?”

“I don’t think that’s the biggest problem here,” he said, and he chuckled again. She looked at him with eyes of thunder. “Don’t worry Mizz Moanalot, they won’t be here long,” Grandpa George said calmly.

“Better not be. I don’t want my petunias getting squashed!!” Grandpa George was a hard man to be cross with so Mizz Moanalot just harrumphed and stomped back into her house to call the police.

The children on the street were loving all the excitement. They climbed on the elephants, stroking them. They particularly liked the little baby elephant with his odd tuft of hair between his floppy ears.

The bonobo ran inside and came out with the telephone.

“Thank you, Charlie,” said Grandpa George. He pressed a few buttons. “Hello Albert, I have some elephants for you. No, I think you’re going to need more than one lorry for this job.” Pause. Nod. “Right.” Pause. Nod. “About fifteen and a baby one if the children on the street don’t kidnap it as a pet first.” Pause. Nod. “Righto Albert. Thank you very much.” Pause. Nod. “See you in about half an hour, then. Cheerio.” He handed the phone back to the bonobo who put it in his mouth and took it back to the house.

Grandpa George then went to talk to the children, explaining to them that these elephants were African elephants because they had big ears and that they belong to the group of animals called pachyderms. This includes other thick-skinned mammals like the rhinoceros and hippopotamus. The children always loved listening to Grandpa George. They especially liked it when he let them come into his house, which was not too often because they were usually more wildly behaved than the animals themselves.

Kiki and the others had heard and seen everything from the hedge they were hiding in.

"Well that-a is-a that-a," declared Piero. "Can-a we go-a homeo now? I'm-a soooo hot in this ridiculoso costume."

"I know what you mean Piero, my head is really itching from this wig," said Kiki.

"Oh, that's probably not the wig," said Dali. "Tiny and Titch tend to fidget when they're waiting. They've been playing rock, paper, scissors. Winston and Churchill have been pacing up and down, too."

"Well, tell them to stop. It tickles."

"So, do we go home now?" asked Banjo.

"I just want to wait until the man from the circus arrives. I've got a funny feeling something is about to happen."

Just then the eye-patch man from the circus turned up yelling.

"Give me me elephants back!" He was shaking his fist. "Them animals is mine." He was talking to Grandpa George and was about to grab him by his collar when all the children from the street stood in front of him, blocking his way. He backed off.

"Listen 'ere mate, I don't know what your game is or who put you up to it, but these 'ere elephants is part of the circus, see," said the eye-patch man.

"No, I don't see. Where are their costumes, then?"

The eye-patch man looked a bit confused. Where had their headdresses gone?

"Never mind that," he said with an evil grin. He pulled out his whip. "If you and yer little chums don't move aside I'll 'ave no other choice but to use this."

Right then, the police turned up. Just one car. Two policemen. Their jaws nearly dropped off when they saw the elephants blocking the road. They thought it had been another hoax call from Mizz Moanalot overreacting.

"Alright, alright, alright," said the bobby. "What seems to be the trouble here?"

"No trouble, officer," said the eye-patch man. "These is me elephants from the circus and I just wanna take em back."

One of the larger elephants pushed the eye-patch man.

"Doesn't seem like they want to come back," said the other policeman.

"What does they know, they're just animals. I looks after em and this man stole em." He pointed his crooked bony finger straight at Grandpa George.

"Now how on earth would a man of my age manage to steal all these animals? I mean really, do I look like Tarzan?" All the children laughed.

Just then a man on stilts, a clown and a bearded belly dancer appeared out of nowhere.

Grandpa George looked at the clown's eyes. I've seen those before he thought to himself. It's that little stray I sent over to my son John. "Your secret is safe with me, Kiki," said Grandpa George to himself. He gave Kiki a nod and she knew that he knew.

The clown shook his finger (in a white glove) at the eye-patch man and then mimicked a person's hand being smacked as if to say bad boy. The clown then pretended to repeatedly kick the eye-patch man on the bottom with his soft floppy shoes.

The children thought it was a great show.

"Doesn't look like you're very popular at the circus, sir," said the first policeman.

"What does he know, he's just a stupid clown," said the eye-patch man.

The clown started jumping around him like a boxer.

"Git away you stupid clown, you're boverin me." He flapped his arms around trying to shove Kiki away, but she was always too quick for him.

"More, more, more," shouted the children. "Get the baddie!"

Kiki carried on her pretend boxing at a 100 miles per hour, fancy footwork and fancy air-punching. She was bouncing around like a kangaroo. Without him noticing, she took his whip. Then she stood still. Face to face with the eye-patch man. Like cowboys at dawn.

She hooked the whip onto her belt. Just like a cowboy ready to shoot, she twitched her fingers around the whip as though at any moment she would grab it and whip him.

The eye-patch man was starting to panic.

"No, no, please don't, you can't the police is ere, this ain't funny anymore," he stuttered.

"No, I don't suppose you'd like to be at this end of the whip," said Grandpa George. "But judging by some of the marks on these elephants, I don't think you've minded being at the other end."

"Right, sir," said the chief policeman. "You're coming with us. Cuff him."

"But you can't do this to me."

"Yes, I can – animal cruelty," said the first police officer.

The younger policeman handcuffed and took him back to the police car.

"And you sir," said the first policeman to Grandpa George. "What exactly are you doing with all these elephants?"

"Ah well, they just came here for a quick medical check before being picked up by the Elephant Foundation." Grandpa George showed him his vet licence.

"Fine, when will that be?" asked the chief policeman.

"He's coming now. You see, there's Albert." A line of huge lorries was making its way down the usually quiet little street. Shocked neighbours peered out of windows. Rarely had they experienced such a commotion.

"And what about you Mr Clown and..." The second policeman looked around for the clown, the man on stilts and the bearded belly dancer, but they had vanished into thin air. All that was left were their costumes on the ground.

Further down the street were three happy cats: one carrying five little mice, one still swinging his hips, and one trying to smooth his fur down after being in a sweaty stilt man costume for too long.

"I'll-a never join a the circus-eo, too sweaty-eo."

"I'm surprised," teased Banjo. "They loved your pia-pia-piano act."

"Ah well you know, we Italianos are natural born performers. What can I say-eo?"

"Such modesty," said Dali.

"What can I say-eo, I'm-a the best at being modesto, too."

They all laughed. It had been a great day: they escaped the Farmies (again) and saved the elephants BIG and small. Time to go home for milkeo and watch the sun set together.

Did you enjoy the story? Bet you're *feline* happy now!

It's not over yet. Look on the next page and find out just how amazing elephants really are with Kiki and Friends.

EleFunFacts Quiz

We learned some stuff in the story about the animals you might find in a circus. Bears, lions, and elephants are fascinating just like cats.

So, let's make this quiz all about those amazing elephants that got rescued. Ready to test your animal instincts?

Are you feline claw-ver? Take the quiz!

Answers are listed further on, so no peeking.

QUESTIONS

1. Which elephant species has the biggest ears?

a. African

b. Asian

2. What is the world's largest land animal?

a. Rhinoceros

b. Elephants

c. Giraffes

3. Elephants take dust and mud baths to keep their skin clean

a. True

b. False

4. An elephant never forgets.

a. True

b. False

5. Elephants are part of which family?

a. Pachyderms

b. Reptiles

c. Herbivores

6. How do elephants communicate?

a. By phone, letter and text

b. Vibrations, trumpet calls, body language, touch and scent

c. Drawing in the mud

d. Talking

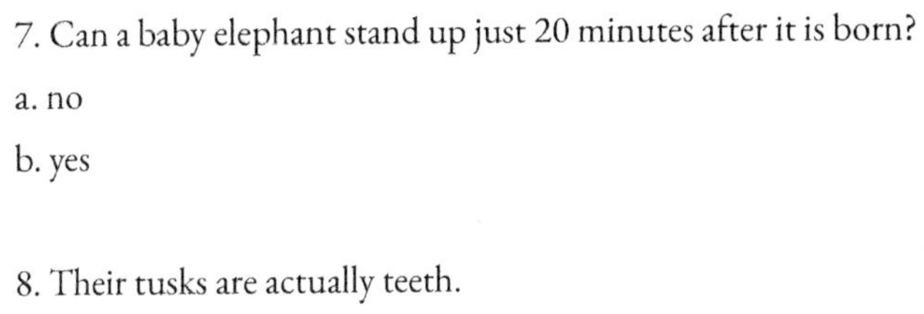

7. Can a baby elephant stand up just 20 minutes after it is born?

a. no

b. yes

8. Their tusks are actually teeth.

a. True

b. False

9. Elephants can laugh.

a. True

b. False

10. What do elephants use their trunk for (choose 2 answers)

a. Sucking up water to drink it

b. To scratch their back

c. To hang off trees

d. As a snorkel when swimming

ANSWERS

1. a African elephants have much larger ears.

2. b

3. True (it also helps to protect them from sunburn!)

4. True – the part of its brain that is used for remembering stuff is loads bigger than ours!

5. a

6. b – of course!

7. Yes! and after just 1 hour it can walk – it takes humans 9 to 15 months!

8. a – True

9. a – True, they can even cry and play!

10. a + d (clever). They can even use it to pick up their baby elephant or a little flower!

So how did you do? Was it a cat-astrophe or are you paw-some?

If you got 5 – 6 out of 10 right, you're pretty clued up.

If you got 7 – 8 out of 10 right, you're a real cat expert.

And 9 or 10 out of 10.... well you're the top cat!!

A NOTE FROM THE AUTHOR

Dear Pawsome Reader

I hope you've enjoyed the story and been inspired to sing life like a song or do a good deed and help someone in need!!

For more free resources and online video courses where you can continue learning with Kiki and her friends visit: www.kikiandfriends.co.uk

As a freelance author I rely on my readers to support me in creating more fun books, journals and instructional videos. I do all the work myself from the idea to the editing, cover design, formatting and marketing—even some of the illustrating! I thoroughly enjoy it and would like to do more.

HOW YOU CAN HELP

You already helped by choosing this book. Could I also ask that you leave a kind review to help guide others to these amazing stories and characters?

Thank you very much. Every good review and recommendation is a step closer to another Kiki adventure being created.

Fuzzy furry thanks!

Francesca Hepton

YOU'VE READ THE BOOK. YOU'VE MET KIKI AND HER FRIENDS.

IT DOESN'T HAVE TO END HERE.
KIKI AND FRIENDS
ARE ONLINE!

JOIN THEM FOR
A NEW STORY or FUN ACTIVITY.

Colouring in
Word searches
Spot the difference
... and much more!

www.kikiandfriends.co.uk

Printed in Great Britain
by Amazon